By Margaret G. Otto

Cover design by Phillip Colhouer
Cover illustration by Barbara Cooney, recreated by Nada Serafimovic
Inside Illustrations by Barbara Cooney
This unabridged version has updated grammar and spelling.

First published in 1954

www.goodandbeautiful.com

For

ANNE PAULINE MARVEL

and her marvelous

pumpkin, ginger, and spice-

colored dachshunds.

Table of Contents

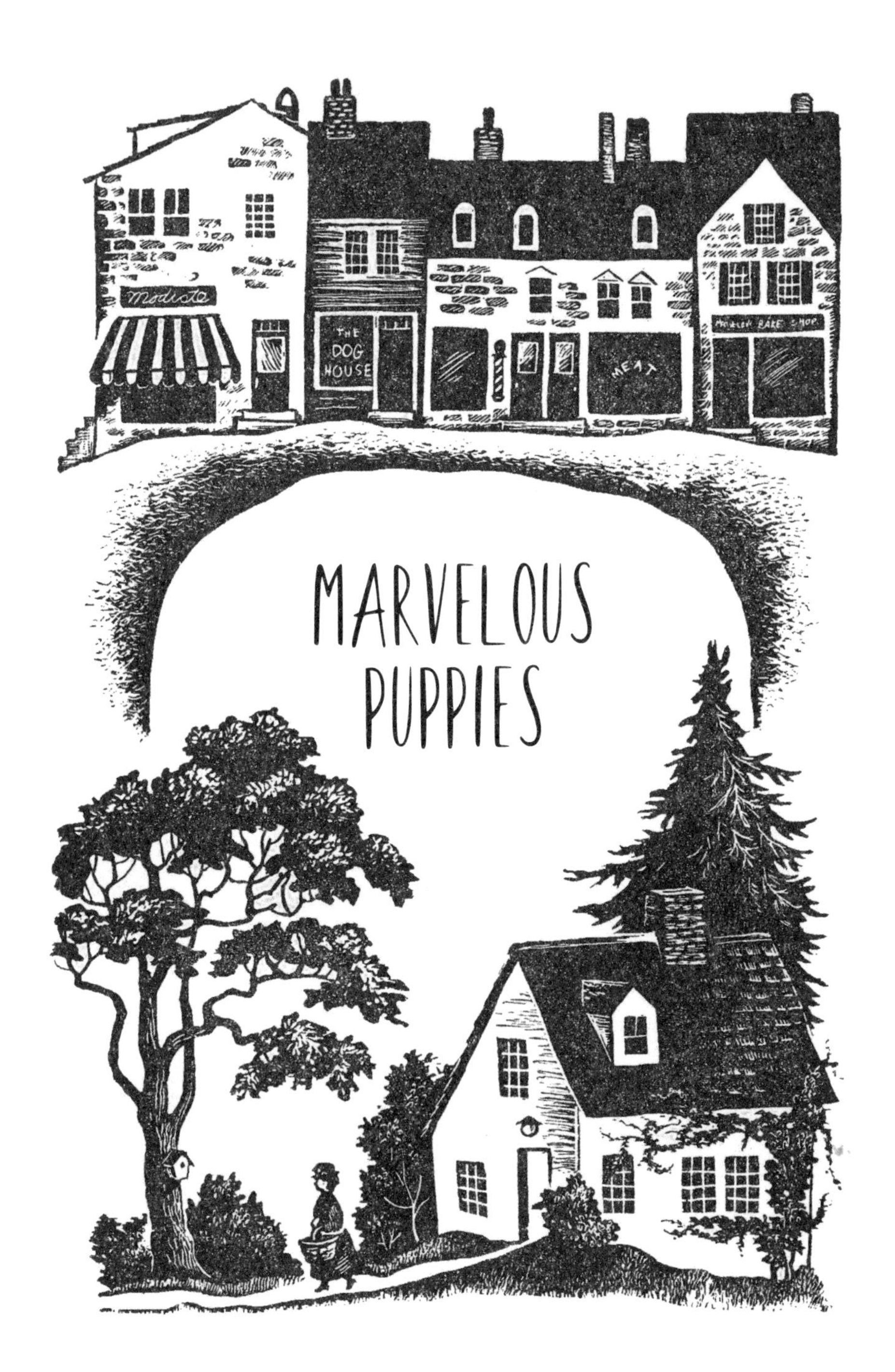
Modiste
THE DOG HOUSE
MEAT
BAKE SHOP
MARVELOUS PUPPIES

Chapter 1

Pumpkin, Ginger, and Spice were three little puppies. They had very long bodies and very short legs and very thin tails. They were dachshunds.

They belonged to Miss Marvelous, the smiling lady who ran the village bake shop. She had given them their brown, tasty names because Pumpkin was the color of pumpkin pie. Ginger was the color of ginger cookies. Spice was the color of spice cake.

Everybody in the village thought Miss Marvelous was marvelous—so were the cakes and cookies and pies in the Marvelous Bake Shop, and so were the three little brown puppies that matched them.

Pumpkin, Ginger, and Spice lived with Miss Marvelous in a white house on Main Street, around two corners from the bake shop. They had come to live with her when they were only three months old. They had lived with her a whole month, so now they were four months old.

The puppies slept together in a basket-bed with a cushion inside. They all ate together from the same bowl. They drank together from the same shiny pail.

"When Pumpkin, Ginger, and Spice grow up, they will each have a basket-bed and bowl and pail," Miss Marvelous told visitors. "And they're each going to have a different color harness with a leash to match."

Pumpkin, Ginger, and Spice were too little to go walking yet. They were also too little to leave at home all day while Miss Marvelous worked at the bake shop. So the first morning after they came, and every day since, she had packed them carefully into a big market basket to take with her.

She packed all their heads at one end and their tails at the other. Then she covered everything but their heads with half of an old brown blanket. The basket was big, and the puppies were small and so far down in the bottom that the basket looked empty. Nobody could tell that Pumpkin, Ginger, and Spice were inside unless he looked over the edge and saw their shiny eyes watching from below.

Everybody who passed Miss Marvelous on her way to the bake shop looked over the edge, so it took her almost twice as long to get there when she was carrying the basket with her little dachshunds inside.

After their bumpy basket ride, Pumpkin, Ginger, and Spice liked to stretch their legs and necks when Miss Marvelous lifted them out onto the floor of the small room behind the bake shop.

In one corner there was a wooden box lined with the other half of the old brown blanket. Here the puppies snuggled up against each other. It was just as soft and warm as their basket-bed in the kitchen of the white house on Main Street, even if it was not as pretty.

"This is your room," Miss Marvelous had said out loud to Pumpkin, Ginger, and Spice the first morning she took them there.

She lifted the puppies out of the market basket in the small room behind her bake shop.

"Some people don't like dogs and pies and

cakes and cookies in the same place. You mustn't come out into the bake shop up front," Miss Marvelous added.

Pumpkin, Ginger, and Spice looked up at her while she was talking, so she knew they were listening to her voice. She knew, too, that she would have to do something to help the puppies learn not to go into the bake shop. They would need to be reminded over and over again. So Miss Marvelous put a big box in the doorway to keep them from getting through.

A few days later, she said to Miss Jennie, her helper in the bake shop, "I'll get Mr. Silver to make a low gate for their door—one we can push open with our feet, but the puppies can't push open with theirs."

The next morning Mr. Silver, the carpenter, came to make a low gate to keep the puppies from getting into the bake shop.

When he started to work, Pumpkin, Ginger, and Spice squeezed themselves together very tightly inside their box. They looked out at him with frightened eyes. After a while, they grew used to the noise he was making with the saw, and they crept out of the box. They began to sniff around the room, as far away from him as they could go.

"When you get to know me, we'll be great friends," said Mr. Silver to the puppies.

There was a look on his face which showed he wanted them to like him.

When he began to hammer, Pumpkin, Ginger, and Spice ran back into their box. They made another tight pile of themselves.

Mr. Silver finished the sawing and hammering. Then he stretched chicken wire between the strips of wood to finish the gate.

"This will keep you in, but you can look out," he said to the dachshunds.

By this time, Pumpkin, Ginger, and Spice were sniffing around Mr. Silver's feet. By the time he had finished the gate, they were licking his hands, and they began playing around in the sawdust and wood shavings he had made on the floor.

"We're friends now," Mr. Silver told Miss Marvelous when she came to look at the gate. "I'll be coming to see them often."

Chapter 2

It was lunchtime for Pumpkin, Ginger, and Spice by the time Mr. Silver had packed his tools and cleared away the sawdust and shavings. While the little puppies were lapping up their lunch, the fire whistle from the firehouse across the street sounded its loud alarm.

"One—two—three—" Miss Marvelous began counting the blasts of the whistle.

"Oh, it's right near here," she cried, running to the front door of the shop, as the whistle sounded over and over again.

Miss Jennie ran outside to look up the street.

At that minute the fire engine rushed out of the firehouse.

"It's Mrs. Moon's hat shop," called Jennie from outside.

"Oh, poor Mrs. Moon! I must go see if I can help her," said Miss Marvelous. "Take care of the shop while I'm gone."

She pulled on her coat and ran out the door, banging it shut behind her.

Miss Jennie stayed outside to watch the excitement of the fire.

Pumpkin, Ginger, and Spice were left alone in the little room at the back of the bake shop. Their three very long bodies scrambled up against the new gate, trying to follow Miss Marvelous. They peered through the wire into the bake shop to watch for her return. They could see people running past the window. Everyone was in a hurry to get to the fire close by.

It was Pumpkin who first smelled smoke. He

started to bark his snappy, small puppy bark. He worked so hard at it that his whole long body moved back and forth with the noise. It was only part of a minute before Ginger and Spice added their puppy barks to Pumpkin's.

When little curls of smoke started to puff through the floor of the back room, Pumpkin's bark grew louder and sharper. Ginger and Spice made their barks sound the same, too! Their short legs and long tails and very long bodies were moving every which way. They kept in time with their barks. More and more curls of smoke puffed through the cracks of the floor in their room.

But nobody was close enough to hear the puppies or to hear their frantic jumping up and down.

Then, Mr. Silver ran by the bake shop.

"The fire's five doors up the street," he called to Miss Jennie out front as he ran past. "All of you at this end of the row are far enough away to be safe."

Pumpkin, Ginger, and Spice tried to bark even harder when they heard Mr. Silver's voice, but he did not hear them.

Next, Pumpkin moved back from the gate a little way and threw himself against it as hard as he could. Ginger and Spice did the same thing. This added a rattling, pounding noise to their fierce little barks.

The man from the shop next door was talking to Miss Jennie as they looked up the street at the fire. He stepped a little closer to the bake shop window. Pumpkin, Ginger, and Spice could see him through the glass. They worked harder and harder to make him hear them.

Suddenly, Pumpkin bumped into a stool that held a pile of tin pie plates. The pie plates came crashing down onto the floor!

Pumpkin, Ginger, and Spice ran to their box and huddled together inside when they heard the noise.

"What's going on in the bake shop?" came the voice of the man from the shop next door. "All that barking and clatter!"

He peered through the window.

All he could see were the little curls of smoke puffing through the floor of the back room and floating up toward the ceiling.

"My soul!" cried the man from the shop next door. "The fire must be creeping along underneath through the cellars! I'll go tell the firemen."

"I'll go get Miss Marvelous," Miss Jennie shouted.

They both rushed up the street, forgetting all about the puppies in their excitement.

Chapter 3

By this time the smoke was swirling slowly all through the little room behind the bake shop. Pumpkin, Ginger, and Spice started to cough. They put their noses close to the floor where there was not so much smoke. They kept running back and forth to the gate.

It seemed like a long time to the three dogs before anybody came, but it was really only a few minutes before two firemen hurried through the front door of the bake shop. A crowd of people followed them as far as the door.

Nobody thought about the little dogs in the back room. They had stopped barking because their noses were choked in smoke.

The door closed behind the firemen. The crowd in front of the window grew bigger. Still Miss Marvelous did not come.

"Where's Miss Marvelous?" a woman called out.

"I saw her helping Mrs. Moon pile up some of the hats," a little boy answered.

"Miss Jennie's looking for her," said another woman as she joined the group.

The loud clanging of another fire engine ended the talking in the crowd. The engine stopped in front of the bake shop.

Just then, Pumpkin, Ginger, and Spice heard a voice calling to them.

"Pumpkin! Ginger! Spice! Oh, my puppies are shut in the back room."

It was Miss Marvelous.

The smoke in the back room was too thick for

Pumpkin, Ginger, and Spice to get enough breath to bark back to her.

Firemen jumped off the fire engine and started into the bake shop.

"You can't come in here, ladies," one of them shouted to Miss Marvelous and Miss Jennie, who were trying to push through the door.

"But my dogs! They're inside, in the back room," cried Miss Marvelous.

"Get the dogs!" two or three people called out at once.

A big hose on the fire engine was unrolled. The firemen pulled it into the bake shop.

The man from the shop next door came up to Miss Marvelous. "When I heard the dogs barking and making such a great noise inside there, I looked in and saw the smoke. They were trying to tell us the fire was spreading way down here. They gave the alarm."

"If only we could hear them now," said Miss Marvelous, "it would help the firemen find

them quickly."

Just the next moment, a fireman came through the door. He had a bundle in his arms.

"Here you are," he said as he handed Miss Marvelous the rug from the floor of the back room. "The puppies were all squeezed together under this rug to try to get away from the smoke. They sure have more sense than a lot of people!"

By this time, Miss Marvelous had unwrapped

the rug around Pumpkin, Ginger, and Spice. She was stroking the little dachshunds to take away the frightened look in their eyes and stop their bodies from trembling.

"Stand back! Let the puppies get some air," Mr. Silver called out.

He pushed through the crowd to be near Pumpkin, Ginger, and Spice.

Just then, the fire chief came out of the bake shop.

"Everything's going to be all right in just a few minutes. It's only the cellar under the back room that started to burn," he said.

"Oh, hurrah! Thank you," Miss Marvelous said.

A tall boy looking through the bake shop window said, "Even the pies and cakes and cookies look all right."

"All of us at this end of the street have the puppies to thank," said the man from the shop next door. "They saved our shops from being badly burned, all right."

"They barked the alarm," Miss Jennie said.

"Whose puppies are they?" asked a stranger.

"They belong to Miss Marvelous, who runs the bake shop," answered a man next to her at the edge of the crowd.

"That means their last name is Marvelous!" another man called out.

"Pumpkin Marvelous, Ginger Marvelous, and Spice Marvelous," explained a little girl who knew them.

"Well, their first names are marvelous, too," said a woman.

This made everybody laugh.

In a few minutes, the firemen were ready to leave the bake shop. They jumped onto the fire engine and went back to their firehouse.

Chapter 4

"Bring the puppies into my shop," said the butcher from the meat shop two doors further down the street. "No smoke got in there. It will be a good place for them to quiet down. Someone go find Mrs. Moon and bring her there, too. I'll make coffee for everybody."

Most of the crowd of people who had gathered to watch the fire were walking away. Miss Marvelous carried Pumpkin, Ginger, and Spice into the meat shop. Several people patted and praised them as she went by.

"I don't suppose you want to stop holding them for even a minute," the butcher said to Miss Marvelous, "but I'll fix a box where they can lie down."

Pumpkin, Ginger, and Spice had stopped breathing hard from all the excitement. Their eyes did not look frightened anymore. The butcher placed a box lined with sawdust close to Miss Marvelous. She put the rug and the puppies inside the box.

Shopkeepers from all along the row crowded into the meat shop. Finally, Mrs. Moon from the hat shop hurried in.

"Things aren't nearly so bad as they might have been," said Mrs. Moon.

She took the cup of coffee the butcher handed her. "I'm grateful that the firehouse is so close," she said. "The firemen got across the street to my shop so fast they were able to save a lot of things. Now, I want to have a good look at the puppies who saved the rest of the shops from being burned."

"Stand aside, everybody!" said a man with a camera who had just come into the meat shop.

"Oh, he wants a picture of Pumpkin, Ginger, and Spice for the newspaper," said Miss Marvelous as she recognized a man from the town newspaper.

She had a proud smile on her face.

The newspaperman leaned over close to Pumpkin, Ginger, and Spice. He took their picture as they snuggled close together inside the box. But they kept watching to make sure Miss Marvelous was nearby.

"They deserve to have their picture in the paper," the butcher said. "And I think we shopkeepers at this end of the row would like you to put something special in the write-up. Say that we're going to give the dogs a present because they saved our shops from burning."

"Yes! Yes! Yes!" agreed all the shopkeepers.

"What shall I say the present is going to be?" asked the newspaperman.

"There are some bright-colored harnesses with leashes to match in the Dog House shop window. That would be a nice present for them," said Miss Jennie.

She had heard Miss Marvelous talk about three red and green and yellow harnesses with leashes to match. She had seen them at the Dog House when she went to buy rubber bones and balls for the puppies. Miss Marvelous often looked in the window and planned what she would like to have for Pumpkin, Ginger, and Spice.

"All right, you can say we're going to give each puppy a harness with a leash to match—a different color for each one," the butcher said.

"Good!" said the newspaperman. He closed his camera and went back to his office.

"Oh, thank you," Miss Marvelous said to the shopkeepers. "You are very kind. These will be the first presents Pumpkin, Ginger, and Spice have ever had, except from me."

When the three little dachshunds heard their names, they jumped out of the box and snuggled close around Miss Marvelous' feet. Their eyes looked happy again—so did their very long bodies and very short legs and very thin tails.

That night when Miss Marvelous put Pumpkin, Ginger, and Spice to bed, she stooped over close to them and said, "Thank you, and there's going to be a harness and a leash for each of you. The red one will be for Pumpkin, the green one for Ginger, and the yellow one for Spice—to match your rubber bones and balls, you see."

The little dogs were fast asleep when she finished explaining and switched off the light.

When Miss Marvelous and the puppies went into the bake shop the next morning, Mr. Silver

rushed in right after them. Pumpkin, Ginger, and Spice wagged their tails when they saw him.

"Look," he said and held out a newspaper to Miss Marvelous.

There was a large picture on the front page.

"Pumpkin, Ginger, and Spice!" she exclaimed.

"Read what it says under the picture," Mr. Silver told her.

Miss Marvelous read the big print out loud: "'MARVELOUS DOGS KEEP CAKE AND MEAT FROM BURNING.' Oh! Isn't that wonderful," she said.

"Wonderful is right!" answered Mr. Silver. "And that makes three more Marvelous cooks in your family."

MARVELOUS DETECTIVES

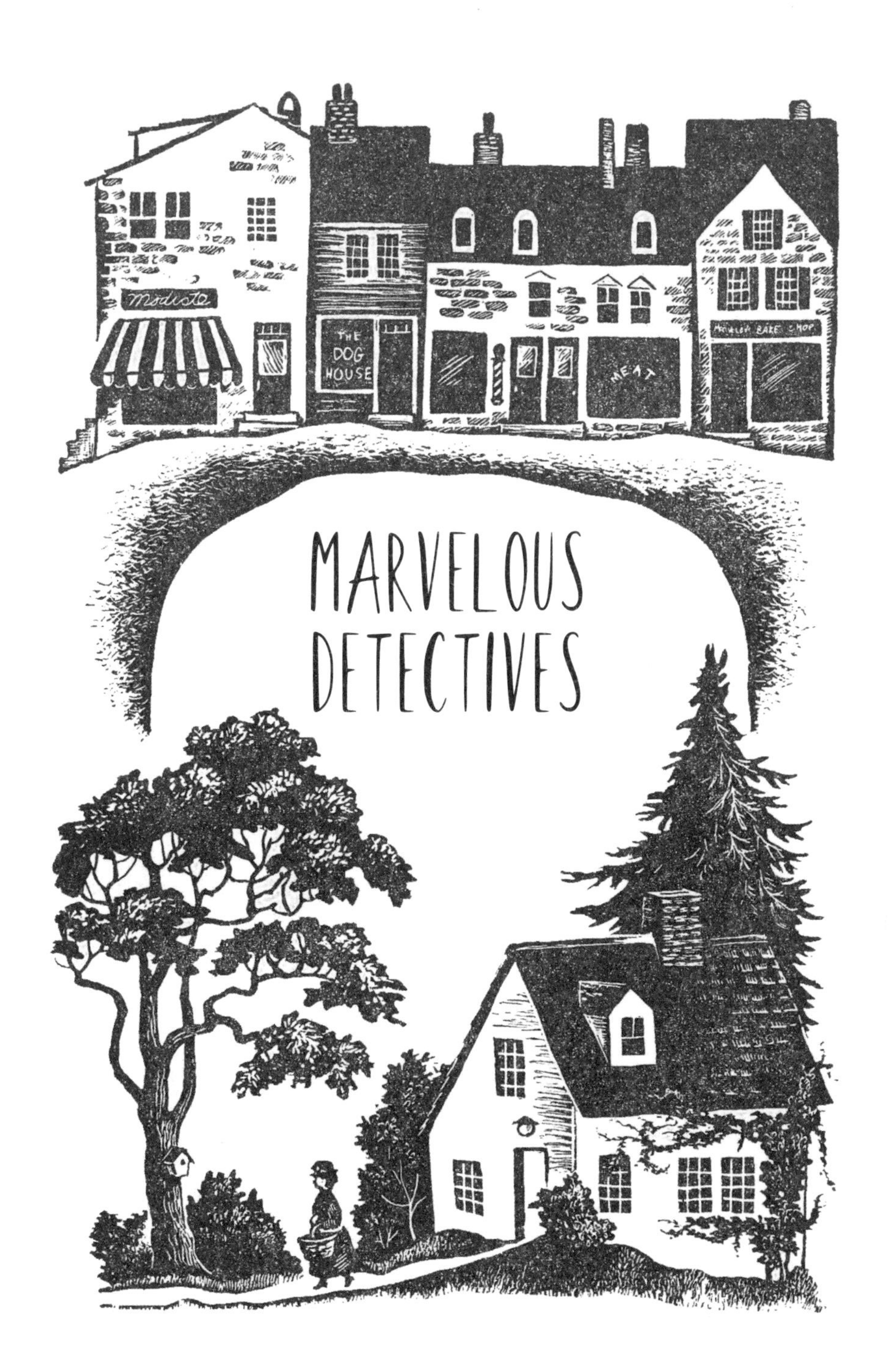

Chapter 1

Pumpkin, Ginger, and Spice had many new visitors after their picture was on the front page of the town newspaper. Girls and boys and grownups, too, wanted to see the puppies with the brown, tasty names.

The visitors all went to the doorway of the little room in back of the bake shop. They stood at the low gate Mr. Silver had made to keep the puppies in. Pumpkin, Ginger, and Spice poked their noses through the chicken wire and wagged their tails to greet them.

"Pumpkin's the one with the red bone," Miss Marvelous explained to a little boy and girl one morning. "Ginger has the green one, and Spice is chewing the yellow one."

"We love their names!" the little girl said. "Mr. Silver often tells us about the puppies. He says they're among his best friends now."

"We're Jack and Polly Bates," explained the little boy. "Mr. Silver taught us the whistle he uses to call the puppies. He made it up himself, and he calls it his Pumpkin-Ginger-and-Spice whistle."

Polly and Jack whistled the short little tune Mr. Silver had taught them. The little brown dogs began to bark and wag their tails and look all around.

"I'm often too busy to listen to all that goes on back here when Mr. Silver stops in to see the puppies," said Miss Marvelous, "but I always hear lots of whistling and talking and barking." Miss Marvelous smiled as she told Polly and Jack this.

"Mr. Silver says you're going to bring Pumpkin,

Ginger, and Spice to his house someday," said Jack.

"We live near him, so he's going to call us over when you come," Polly added.

"That will be nice," said Miss Marvelous. "Ever since my shop neighbors gave the puppies their fine harnesses and leashes, I've been teaching them to walk beside me. They walk to the bake shop with me every morning now! I used to have to carry them in a market basket. Pretty soon they'll be old enough to go as far as Mr. Silver's house over by the river."

"We'll be there, too," Polly and Jack said as they waved to the puppies. "Goodbye, Pumpkin, Ginger, and Spice."

Chapter 2

It was a few weeks later on a sunny Sunday afternoon. Miss Marvelous decided that Pumpkin, Ginger, and Spice were old enough to walk to Mr. Silver's house. When the little brown dogs saw her pick up the harnesses, they came running to have them put on. They wriggled with excitement as she pushed their bodies into the harnesses and fastened on the leashes.

When Miss Marvelous said, "We're going to Mr. Silver's," the three little dogs wagged their tails and began to bark. They knew Mr. Silver's name. He was one of their best friends. He talked and played and whistled in just the ways puppies like best. And the sound of his name made Pumpkin, Ginger, and Spice wag their tails hard with excitement.

Their tails were still wagging as they started off to Mr. Silver's house. They walked proudly beside Miss Marvelous in the direction of the river. Their eyes looked quickly at everything they passed. Their noses sniffed and snuffed from time to time along the way.

Miss Marvelous smiled as she watched their short legs take tiny, fast steps.

She smiled at their thin tails waving out in back.

And she smiled again when she looked at the crowded little path of footsteps they left behind them on the soft road.

"Mr. Silver knows we may be coming to see him today," Miss Marvelous said out loud to Pumpkin, Ginger, and Spice.

The dogs looked up at her when they heard Mr. Silver's name again.

As they turned into the lane that ran along the river, Polly and Jack Bates came running to meet them.

"You're going to Mr. Silver's, aren't you?" Jack asked. "He told us Pumpkin, Ginger, and Spice might be coming today."

"It's the longest walk they've ever taken," said Miss Marvelous. "They'll need to lie down and rest when they get to Mr. Silver's house."

Pumpkin, Ginger, and Spice were walking a little more slowly now. Suddenly Spice sat right down in the middle of the lane.

"She's tired!" said Polly.

"Don't you want us to help you carry them?" asked Jack.

"That's a good idea," said Miss Marvelous. "They mustn't get too tired because they have to walk back home again, too. Let's each carry one of them."

Mr. Silver's house was only a little further away. As they got to the front gate, Pumpkin, Ginger, and Spice began to bark.

"They're calling Mr. Silver," said Miss Marvelous. "Their noses tell them he lives here. Let's put them down and unfasten the leashes."

The puppies rushed along the path as fast as they could run. They scrambled up the steps that led to Mr. Silver's front door. They were barking louder now.

"I wonder why he doesn't come out to meet them," said Jack.

"Maybe he's taking a nap," Miss Marvelous said. "I'll ring the doorbell to wake him up."

So Pumpkin, Ginger, Spice, Miss Marvelous, Polly, and Jack stood waiting for Mr. Silver to answer his doorbell. But nobody came. The door stayed closed, and it was quiet inside the house. The puppies sat down on the top step.

"Mr. Silver was home before lunch," said Polly. "Blackie, the crow, was here, too. He often comes in from the woods to visit. Mr. Silver lets us feed Blackie and play with him a little bit."

"Acorns—that's Mr. Silver's squirrel friend—hopped on the window sill and looked at us while we were here, too. Mr. Silver was very busy," said Jack.

Then with a quick, secret look at Polly he added, "He was busy polishing his collection."

"Polishing his collection?" Miss Marvelous said with a question in her voice.

"Oh, Mr. Silver has a collection of little silver presents that people have been giving him ever since he was born," Jack explained. "There's a little ox, and some teeny-weeny silver toys, and a thimble, and a tiny cup, and some other little things. He stands them on a shelf he made. He says it's his name that gives people the idea of giving him silver presents."

"And he keeps them very shiny," Polly said.

"Well, isn't that interesting!" said Miss Marvelous.

Pumpkin, Ginger, and Spice were sniffing at the front door now.

"You two had better go into the woods a little way and call Mr. Silver. Maybe he's gone to see what this spring sunshine is doing to the buds on the trees," said Miss Marvelous.

She leaned over and fastened the leashes on Pumpkin, Ginger, and Spice so they could not run into the woods, too.

"Mr. Silver! Mr. Silver!" Jack and Polly started to call his name as soon as they ran out of the gate and along the river where the trees grew close together.

Pumpkin, Ginger, and Spice looked up at Miss Marvelous and wagged their tails.

"Mr. Silver will be here in a minute," she assured them.

She had hardly finished saying this when the puppies began to bark loudly.

"Here I am!" Mr. Silver's voice called from the woods as he came walking toward the house. Polly and Jack were each holding one of his hands.

Chapter 3

Pumpkin, Ginger, and Spice wagged and barked and wiggled around Mr. Silver as soon as he reached the door.

"So sorry I wasn't here to say hello when you first came," Mr. Silver said to Miss Marvelous and Pumpkin, Ginger, and Spice.

He patted the puppies and let them lick his hands.

"Pumpkin, Ginger, and Spice were very excited," Miss Marvelous said. "Their noses told them you live here."

"Well, I've had a bit of a bad time," Mr. Silver went on to say. "I've lost my favorite piece in my collection of silver presents."

"Oh, your silver thimble?" asked Polly.

"Yes," said Mr. Silver. "It's the thimble my father gave my mother the day I was born. It has her initials and my initials and my birthday date written inside."

"Oh! That's a very important thimble," said Miss Marvelous. "We must find it. Have you any idea what could have happened?"

"Well, I last saw the thimble while I was cleaning my silver collection before lunch," said Mr. Silver. "I have a habit of shining the thimble first of all the things. Then I put it down on the table in front of me so I can look at it while I'm polishing the rest of the collection."

"It was there when we came to watch you polish to. . ." Polly stopped herself right in the middle of the sentence and popped her hand over her mouth.

". . . when we came to watch you polish your collection," Jack finished the sentence for Polly, with a secret little look in his eyes, "and we fed Blackie, the crow, too."

"Blackie stayed with me while I ate my lunch," Mr. Silver said. "I had to give him some of it, too, you may be sure. I opened the window and gave Acorns some nuts for his Sunday lunch. It was warm, so I left the window open. Blackie and Acorns are used to being that close to each other now. But they aren't friends, so I can't have them both inside at the same time. While I was talking to them, a terrible noise suddenly came from the flock of crows in the woods. Acorns whisked away from the window sill. Blackie flew out the window. I ran after them to see what it was all about."

"We heard the crows," said Jack, "but we were eating lunch, and Mother wouldn't let us go out to see what was the matter."

"Well, the crows were all excited and upset. I figured a squirrel must have got into a nest and stolen the eggs. It was a commotion all right!"

"Was the thimble gone when you got back to your house?" Polly asked.

"Well now, I can't be sure," said Mr. Silver. "I didn't put my silver collection back on its shelf until I'd cleared away my lunch dishes. That's when I first missed the thimble. I've moved everything in the room to see whether it rolled off the table. But it isn't anywhere."

While Mr. Silver was talking, Pumpkin, Ginger, and Spice were sniffing around the room.

"They're hunting for your thimble, Mr. Silver," Polly said.

"Good! Just like three little detectives," said Mr. Silver.

When the puppies came to the open window, they began to jump and bark a little.

"They smell your squirrel friend, Mr. Silver," said Miss Marvelous. "They're just getting to know squirrels, you see."

"Then they probably want to go outside and find more of them," said Mr. Silver. "Why not let them go for a run in our woods? I don't want to spoil their visit just because I've lost my silver thimble."

Chapter 4

Mr. Silver led the way out of the house. Pumpkin, Ginger, and Spice looked at Miss Marvelous quickly to make sure it was all right for them to run off. Then they tore away into the woods with their ears and tails waggling as they ran.

Polly and Jack ran after them. Two squirrels hurried across their path and whisked up a tall tree to get out of the way.

"When you and the dogs arrived, I was looking around in the woods," explained Mr. Silver. "I thought I might have taken the thimble with me when I went out to see what had frightened the crows. I do sometimes wear it on this little finger."

"Oh, do you think that might have happened?" asked Miss Marvelous. "We had all better hunt around carefully then."

"The crows were making the noise near this big tree," said Mr. Silver. He pointed to a large oak tree on his left.

Miss Marvelous began to look carefully on the ground. She hunted all around where Mr. Silver might have stood to look up at the crows. Pumpkin, Ginger, Spice, Polly, and Jack had gone a little farther into the woods.

"Mr. Silver!" Jack called in a minute. "We think we see Blackie sitting on a branch over here. He looks as though he knows us, too."

Just then there was a scuffle in the tree above where the crow was sitting. He flew off the branch and was joined first by one crow and then by

three or four. All of them were cawing loudly and wildly.

"Whew! A squirrel must be trying to steal their eggs again," cried Mr. Silver as a bushy squirrel tail waved at one end of a branch high in the tree. "I wonder if it's Blackie's nest that's being robbed."

Pumpkin, Ginger, and Spice came running over. For a moment, the barking of the dogs and the cawing of the crows and the clucking of the squirrel made a great commotion. Then the squirrel jumped across to another tree, and still another tree, and disappeared among the leaves farther off. The crows stopped their cawing.

Pumpkin, Ginger, and Spice ran off in the direction the big squirrel had gone. It was only a moment before their sharp barks, with a new sound in them now, came from someplace deeper in the woods.

Miss Marvelous and Mr. Silver followed Jack and Polly to the place where the dogs had stopped. Pumpkin, Ginger, and Spice kept looking up into the tree above and then down to the ground. They pushed their noses among the leaves for a minute. Suddenly, Polly saw something very bright lying on the ground.

"It's Mr. Silver's silver thimble!" Polly cried out. She picked up the shiny object.

"Well now!" exclaimed Mr. Silver. "Pumpkin, Ginger, and Spice have found my thimble for me."

"Let's see," said Jack.

Miss Marvelous was patting the little dogs and fastening on their leashes again. She looked very proud.

"What could have happened?" she asked Mr. Silver.

"Guess I know what happened, all right," Mr.

Silver replied. "I didn't even want to think about it before, but I can't help it now."

"What happened, Mr. Silver? Tell us!" said Jack and Polly, almost together.

"Well, that rascal crow, Blackie, must have stolen my thimble from the table and carried it off to his nest. The squirrel we saw thought it was an egg and took it away with him. Then Pumpkin, Ginger, and Spice frightened the squirrel. So he dropped the thimble, and the puppies nosed it out down here in the leaves. That's the story!" finished Mr. Silver.

"Oh," said Polly, "would Blackie do that?"

"Yes, crows love bright things. They steal them from time to time. Blackie doesn't know it's wrong, I'm sure," said Mr. Silver with special loyalty in his voice for his crow friend. "Well now, we must have a party for the Marvelous puppy detectives. My thimble might have been lost forever if they hadn't found it."

Chapter 5

In a few minutes, Pumpkin, Ginger, Spice, Miss Marvelous, Polly, and Jack were all back with Mr. Silver in his house. First, Mr. Silver put the thimble back in its place on the silver collection shelf. Then he showed Miss Marvelous each of the shiny silver presents standing in a row. Pumpkin, Ginger, and Spice lay quietly resting in one corner of the room.

"Now for a party in honor of the puppy detectives!" Mr. Silver said, clapping his hands together.

Pumpkin, Ginger, and Spice jumped up from the corner and followed him into the kitchen.

In a minute, Mr. Silver was busy scooping ice cream from a pan he took out of the icebox. He put a tiny scoopful in each of three saucers lined up on the kitchen table. Then he made high piles of ice cream on four big blue plates. Everybody helped carry them into the living room.

"There isn't any newspaperman around to take their picture, the way there was after the fire," said Mr. Silver as he looked at the puppies. "So I'll draw a picture of them instead. Then Miss Marvelous will have something to remind her of the day the silver thimble was lost and then found by her three smart little dogs."

Mr. Silver put down his plate of ice cream and went across the room to the desk. He took out a large piece of paper and a pencil. Miss Marvelous and Polly and Jack watched him make a quick drawing of Pumpkin, Ginger, and Spice, who were lapping up their ice cream. He drew a picture of the thimble down in one corner, too. He made it much bigger than it really was because it was so important.

"Oh, that's wonderful! It looks just like them," Miss Marvelous exclaimed as Mr. Silver handed her the drawing. "I'm going to have it framed and hang it in the bake shop where lots of people can see it."

Polly and Jack kept looking very hard at Mr. Silver. They made secret signals to him when Miss Marvelous wasn't looking.

"I know what you two are thinking about," said Mr. Silver at last. He had a big smile on his face. "You're wondering whether all this excitement has made me forget the surprise, aren't you?"

Jack and Polly shook their heads to say, "Yes."

Everybody was finished eating ice cream by this time.

Mr. Silver gathered the plates together and gave them to Polly to take to the kitchen. He followed her out of the living room. Pumpkin, Ginger, and Spice made a little parade of themselves and followed Mr. Silver.

Polly came back through the kitchen door. Her arms were full of Pumpkin, Ginger, and Spice.

"Mr. Silver wants them in here with you," she said to Miss Marvelous.

As Polly walked through the sunlight, which was coming from the window, little bright beams of light darted from the harnesses around the puppies.

"Oh! What's that shining on their harnesses?" Miss Marvelous asked excitedly.

She rushed over to Pumpkin, Ginger, and Spice. There on each harness was fastened a bright silver tag.

The one on Pumpkin's red harness said: PUMPKIN MARVELOUS, 25 MAIN STREET, WESTVILLE, CONN. And Miss Marvelous' telephone number was in one corner.

Ginger's name and address and telephone number were on the little silver tag attached to his green harness.

Spice's name and address and telephone number were on a silver tag on her yellow harness.

"Silver name tags!" exclaimed Miss Marvelous.

"That's in case the puppies get lost," said Jack.

"Or in case anybody wants to know what their names are," added Polly.

Mr. Silver was quiet and smiling.

"Mr. Silver made them all by himself," Polly said.

"That's what we were really watching him polish this morning," Jack said. "Polly almost told you, Miss Marvelous. But she caught herself in time, before she gave away the surprise. So we pretended we were watching him polish his silver collection. But he really didn't do that until after we'd gone home."

"It's a wonderful surprise! Thank you, Mr. Silver. Oh, thank you!" Miss Marvelous said. "Real silver name tags for Pumpkin, Ginger, and Spice," she murmured as she read the names and addresses again.

"I guess my name always makes me think about silver things," said Mr. Silver.

"And silver things always make me think about your name," said Miss Marvelous.

"Me, too," Jack and Polly said together.

"It's a bright, shiny name," added Polly.

"Just like silver," said Jack.

Everybody laughed.

"We must go home now," said Miss Marvelous. "We've had a wonderful afternoon! And we all love our presents."

She patted the picture that Mr. Silver had rolled up for her to carry. She looked down at the silver name tags, put on her coat, and fastened the three leashes to the harnesses on her puppies.

"We wish that you and Pumpkin, Ginger, and Spice lived here," Polly said.

"Please come again soon," said Mr. Silver.

Then everyone said goodbye.

Miss Marvelous waved as she went through the gate with the puppies.

Mr. Silver and Polly and Jack waved back from the steps.

"I'll see you tomorrow on my way home from work," Mr. Silver called out to the little brown dogs as they went down the lane.

The puppies barked a friendly answer when they heard Mr. Silver's voice.

Just then the sun caught the light on the three silver name tags. They made Pumpkin, Ginger, and Spice look very important.

"Oh, look!" Jack called out. "Their name tags shine just like real detectives' badges."

"They are real detectives. Marvelous detectives," said Mr. Silver.

MARVELOUS DOGS

Chapter 1

Pumpkin, Ginger, and Spice were a year old one Saturday in June. Miss Marvelous tied a red ribbon on Pumpkin, a green ribbon on Ginger, and a yellow ribbon on Spice. Their silver name tags were shining brightly.

Miss Marvelous had invited Mr. Silver and Polly and Jack to a birthday party.

Pumpkin, Ginger, and Spice heard them as they came up the walk. They were all whistling the Pumpkin-Ginger-and-Spice whistle. Then the front door opened.

"Happy birthday! Happy birthday! Happy birthday!" their three voices sang out as they came inside.

"That's a happy birthday for each one of you," Jack explained as he patted the dogs.

Pumpkin, Ginger, and Spice seemed to be everywhere at once—rubbing against Mr. Silver, licking Polly's hands, and barking friendly little barks around Jack's feet. They came back to Miss Marvelous in between to show her they were glad she was there, too.

"We have presents they can open themselves," said Polly as she hopped up and down with excitement.

"Here's mine!" said Jack. He laid a very lumpy white package on the floor.

Pumpkin snatched it first. Then Ginger and Spice both grabbed the other end with their teeth. They all pulled. The soft white tissue paper tore off easily, and out rolled three rubber hot dogs!

"Hot dogs!" cried Miss Marvelous. "They look

as though they would taste like real ones, too. Oh, thank you, Jack."

Polly laid three separate packages on the floor. One was tied with red ribbon, one with green ribbon, and one with yellow ribbon.

"Red's for Pumpkin, green's for Ginger, and yellow's for Spice—the way it always is," Polly said as she put the packages in front of each dog.

The little dogs chewed off the ribbons and paper in a jiffy. Each one found a rubber bone inside, the same color as the ribbon around the package.

"How wonderful, Polly," Miss Marvelous said, as excited as if it were her own birthday present. "They need new rubber bones badly. They've chewed their first ones to bits since their teeth have grown so much bigger."

Pumpkin carried his bone and his hot dog into the basket-bed and sat down beside them. Ginger and Spice copied him. They were very crowded.

"Here's a brown paper bag for your birthday present, my friends," Mr. Silver said with a secret in his voice. He put the bag down on the floor. It stood up by itself because it was very full.

Pumpkin, Ginger, and Spice tumbled out of the basket-bed. They sniffed and snuffed and sniffed. They began to bark and scratch at the bag. It fell over.

Pumpkin put his head into the open end. Ginger and Spice squeezed theirs in, too.

Everybody laughed. For a moment, the dogs snuffed and puffed with their heads inside the bag. Then—the paper split open. Up came their heads. And in each mouth was a small net bag, full of dog candy.

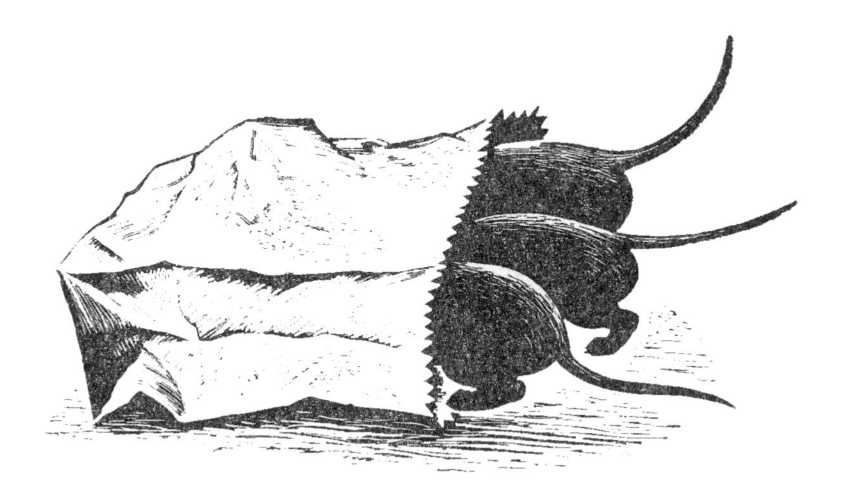

"Oh, they love dog candy!" Miss Marvelous exclaimed with a big smile. "Santa Claus brought them some for Christmas."

She picked a piece from each net bag and gave them to her little brown dogs.

"You may each have one piece," she said.

"Mr. Silver took us to the Dog House to do our shopping," explained Polly.

"I did mine there, too," said Miss Marvelous.

She opened the door of the closet in one corner of the room. It was a big closet and very dark. For a moment there were busy sounds after Miss Marvelous disappeared inside. Then, she came out carrying a pile of new basket-beds—one, two, three.

She went back into the closet and brought out three shiny drinking pails and three eating bowls—a red one, a green one, and a yellow one.

Pumpkin, Ginger, and Spice jumped up and down all around her, barking as loud as they could.

"You're too big to fit into one bed comfortably or to eat and drink together from one dish," Miss Marvelous said.

She set the three basket-beds in a row along one wall of the hall.

She lifted Pumpkin into the first one, which had a red cushion. She lifted Ginger into the second one, which had a green cushion. Spice jumped into the third one, which had a yellow cushion.

"Look," Polly cried, "Spice knows her own color now!"

"Don't they look nice in their new beds?" said Mr. Silver.

"Now come into the dining room for the rest of the birthday party," said Miss Marvelous.

She picked up the dogs' new eating bowls and led the way. Pumpkin, Ginger, and Spice jumped out of their new beds and hurried in, too.

"Oh!" cried Polly when she saw the table set for the birthday party.

"Everything's red, green, and yellow for Pumpkin, Ginger, and Spice."

There were paper streamers hanging down from the light to the sides of the table. And there was a tablecloth made of red, green, and yellow strips of paper. On the floor lay a small paper tablecloth, just like the one on the big birthday-party table.

"Well now!" Mr. Silver said, "Pumpkin, Ginger, and Spice have their own little birthday-party table set for them on the floor."

Then Miss Marvelous let Polly help her in the kitchen.

"You put a tiny mound of ice cream in each new bowl for the dogs," she said, "and I'll pile up a big mountain of ice cream on each plate for the people." Then she carried the bowls and the plates to the dining room.

"Excuse me a minute," Miss Marvelous said with a mysterious smile. She went into the kitchen again. It was only a few moments before she was back. Her eyes were very bright from the light of three candles on the big birthday cake she was carrying.

"Oh, look!" shouted Polly. "It's really three cakes all in one."

"Whew!" said Jack. "One part has red icing, another part's green, and the other part's yellow—with a candle to match each part."

"That's for Pumpkin. That's for Ginger. That's for Spice," Polly said as she pointed out the three colors.

"Bet I know whose idea it was," Mr. Silver said. He looked right at Miss Marvelous.

"Yes, I made their birthday cake," she said quietly.

"This is the best birthday party I've ever been to," said Mr. Silver.

"Me too," Jack and Polly said at the same time.

Pumpkin, Ginger, and Spice had never been to any other birthday party. They barked and jumped up against Miss Marvelous to show how exciting they thought it was.

Polly and Jack whispered together for a minute. Then, they made a secret wish for the three little dogs before they blew out the candles with one big puff.

"You'll get the wish soon," Polly said to the dogs. Then she whispered to Miss Marvelous, "We made them wish they could play detectives in our woods with Blackie, the crow, and Acorns again. Wouldn't it be wonderful if they found something else as exciting as the silver thimble?"

"Now we've had two ice cream parties with Pumpkin, Ginger, and Spice," said Jack.

"Wonder when we'll have the next?" asked Polly.

After the party was all over, and Mr. Silver and Polly and Jack had gone home, Miss Marvelous said out loud to Pumpkin, Ginger, and Spice, "Now you're a whole year old."

The dogs gazed up at Miss Marvelous while she talked to them. They even looked more grown-up.

"You're grown-up enough to be watchdogs now," she went on to say. "So you will be staying here to take care of the house, instead of coming to the bake shop with me."

From then on Pumpkin, Ginger, and Spice watched over the white house on Main Street while their mistress worked at the bake shop.

When Miss Marvelous was at the bake shop, the brown pies and cookies and cakes made her think of the three well-browned dogs at home. And when she was at home, Pumpkin, Ginger, and Spice made her think of the good things to eat at the bake shop.

Being watchdogs kept Pumpkin, Ginger, and Spice very busy. Every time they heard someone coming along the street, they had to scramble from the footstool to the window seat. Then they had to bark and wave their tails until whoever it was had gone away.

Between times they chased each other, rolled on the dining room rug, played with their rubber toys, and, of course, they often went to sleep, even in the daytime. But they were always awake to greet Miss Marvelous when she came home to see them at lunchtime.

Chapter 7

One hot summer day, Miss Marvelous could not stay with them as long as usual when she came home at lunchtime. She had to hurry back to the bake shop to make an extra large birthday cake that had been ordered for a party. In her hurry, she forgot to make sure the screen door had clicked shut behind her.

At first, the dogs did not notice that the door was a tiny bit open. They were busy on the window seat watching Miss Marvelous go away. It was Spice who found out later when a ball rolled into the front hall and she ran after it. She sniffed and scratched at the door. Pumpkin and Ginger came to help her. All three pushed and wriggled and pushed until the door opened wide enough to let them squeeze through.

Then the little brown dogs were off! Of course they liked their nice white house, but best of all they liked to be wherever Miss Marvelous was. So they headed for the bake shop. They knew the way around two corners because they had been there so often.

Down Main Street they went and around the two corners one by one, noses to the ground and tails in the air—Pumpkin, Ginger, and Spice in a little dachshund parade. But they weren't dressed up for a parade because their harnesses were hanging on a doorknob at home.

Suddenly, Pumpkin stopped and raised his head, sniffing hard.

Behind him, Ginger and Spice stopped, too, and raised their heads and sniffed. All three tails began to swing from side to side. Then, before you could say "cookie," they ran across the street and climbed into a car. It was parked in front of the five-and-ten, with one back door standing partly open.

On the floor of the car stood a large basket full of packages, beach bags, and a paper box tied with string. The box had "Marvelous Bake Shop" printed on the top.

One by one the three little dogs jumped into the basket and sniffed at the box. It was warm, and it smelled—marvelous! Their noses had led them right to it. But this was not the bake shop! Miss Marvelous was not there.

"Sniff, sniff, sniff," they went, feeling puzzled and wondering what to do next.

Suddenly the back door of the car slammed shut. Then the front door opened, and someone climbed into the driver's seat.

"Come, Jimmie," said a woman's voice. "We'll have to hurry to get home because Daddy's coming earlier today. Call Sally away from that shop window and jump into the car, both of you, as fast as you can."

The three little dogs were frightened. They huddled together among the packages and lay very still.

"This time I want to come in front with you and Jimmie," said a little girl's voice.

"All right," her mother answered. "Now we'll see if you two can tell the way home from here yet."

Sally said slowly, "It's only the third time we've

been shopping in Westville with you, but I think we turn left at the traffic light."

"Then we go around a curve in front of that little red house," her brother broke in.

Pumpkin, Ginger, and Spice did not stir or make a sound. They had never ridden in a car before. When it started they felt strange, as though a house were moving.

As the car traveled on and on, they could hear the people talking in the front seat, but none of the voices belonged to Miss Marvelous or to anyone they knew.

They were lost and frightened. So Pumpkin licked Ginger, Ginger licked Spice, Spice licked Pumpkin, and they were a little comforted.

By and by the car came to a full stop.

"Everybody carry something into the house," said the children's mother as they all got out. "Sally can take the beach bags and hang up the bathing suits. Jimmie, you help me bring in the rest of the things."

Sally opened the back door of the car and,

without really looking, reached into the basket. Instead of a beach bag, her hand came upon something warm and smooth and plump! It squirmed a little.

Sally jumped and gave a squeal. "Mother! Jimmie!" she cried. "Quick! Quick! Come here. Come see."

There in the basket were the three dogs gazing with sad, anxious eyes.

"Oh! Where did they come from? Whose are they? Can we keep them? How did they get in the car?" asked Jimmie, bursting with excitement.

"They must have jumped in while we were having our ice cream," answered his mother. "I remember the door was left open. But where on earth did they come from? We don't know anyone around here yet."

"First load into the house is a dog apiece," said Sally happily.

"Yes," said Mother, "the screened porch will be

a good place for them until we can find out who they belong to."

Each picked up a dog and carried it to the screened porch and put it down on the floor.

Chapter 3

Pumpkin, Ginger, and Spice gathered together in a tight little bunch. They looked timidly around. There were no basket-beds to crawl into, no rug to roll on, no bright bowls with dinner waiting, no rubber toys to play with, and no Miss Marvelous! It was not home.

"If we give them some dinner right away, maybe they won't feel so lost and lonely," said Sally.

She tried to comfort the three little dogs, patting two at a time in turns.

"Hello, Sally and Jim, what's new?" said a man's voice.

Their father came out onto the porch.

Jimmie ran to him proudly. "There is something new today, Daddy! Look what we found in the car just now when we got home from the beach!"

Then everybody began to talk at once, telling Mr. Henry what had happened and asking questions.

"We'll have to find their owner as soon as we can," he said. "Somebody is worrying about them this very minute. We must let the police know right away that we have them here safe and sound. I'll phone the Westville police station." And he went into the house.

"But we can keep them overnight, can't we?" asked Sally.

"Maybe nobody will miss them for a few days . . . maybe never!" said Jimmie. "Then we'd have three dogs of our own for always, wouldn't we?"

His mother smiled. "Don't think so far ahead," she said. "Let's just wait and see. Now both of you go bring the things from the car while I find something for their dinner."

Sally looked at the sad-eyed brown dogs still quietly huddled together.

"I wish they didn't seem so unhappy," she said. "Perhaps they will feel better when they've had something to eat."

When Sally brought in the box from the bake shop, all three dogs stood up, whimpering, and followed her across the porch.

"Oh, look!" said Mother. "They smell the cookies! They must like them. Don't you think we could each spare one for their dessert?"

"They can have all of mine," said Jimmie.

"Mine, too," said Sally.

Father came back from the telephone.

"There," he said, "I've told the police station we've found three dogs. The officer said no one has reported any lost dogs yet, but people often go looking themselves for their pets before they call the police. They try to think of all the places that they might run away to, you know. I told the officer we would keep them here overnight anyway."

"Suppose nobody calls the police?" asked Sally. "Suppose the dogs were in a car that just happened to be passing through the village, and they jumped out while the driver was in a shop. And he didn't know it. What then? Would they belong to us?"

"I'm afraid not," said Father. "You see, even if anything like that had happened, the driver would probably get in touch with the police or advertise or something. So we'll just have to wait and see."

Mother said, "It looks as though they've run away. They have no collars or harnesses or licenses on, but they look so well cared for they must belong to someone."

"You've both been wanting a dog for a long time, haven't you?" asked Father.

"Oh yes!" cried Sally and Jimmie.

"And we've been thinking about getting one for you. But three! That's different—that would be two too many. Besides, these dogs certainly want to go back to their own home. Did you ever see sadder little creatures? They look as though tears might stream down their faces any minute."

Dinner that night was on the cool screened porch. But no one seemed to want to eat very much. The family were too excited about the strange dogs to feel hungry. And the dogs were too excited about the strange family.

"I wish we knew their names," said Sally. "If only we could call them by their names, they might feel more at home."

"Let's try," said Jimmie. "Brownie! Here Brownie!"

"Penny!" said Mother. "Nice Penny! Good dog."

"Lady!" said Father. "Sweet little Lady. Here Lady."

But nothing happened. The three dachshunds stayed huddled in their corner and paid no attention.

"Oh dear," said Sally, "we'll never be able to guess!"

There was applesauce for dessert, and with it was a big plate of ginger cookies from the bake shop. As soon as the dogs caught a whiff of the Marvelous Bake Shop smell, they lifted their sharp noses into the air, sniffing hopefully.

"Why, look!" said Jimmie. "They seem happier. It's the cookies. They smell them. They must love ginger."

"They're the color of ginger themselves," remarked Sally.

Ginger pricked up his ears, and suddenly his eyes looked eager.

"To me, they seem more the color of spice cake," said Mother.

Spice sat up and put her head on one side.

"They remind me of pumpkin pie," said Father.

Pumpkin stood up on his short legs and took a step forward. All three long tails began to wag shyly and hopefully.

"Now they seem to want to make friends!" exclaimed Sally.

"Yes, suddenly they're interested," said Father. "Do you suppose they understood something we said?"

"What could it have been?" cried Jimmie.

Everybody wondered. But of course, no one could guess that the little dogs had heard their very own names. The three long tails stopped their timid wagging, and Pumpkin, Ginger, and Spice lay down again in their corner, looking even sadder than before.

At bedtime, Sally and Jimmie did their best to make the dachshunds comfortable. They brought three cushions and three bowls of water and patted each little dog goodnight. Then they went quietly away.

But all this did no good. Pumpkin, Ginger, and Spice could not settle down. They knew they did not belong in this strange, dark place. They wanted their own cushions and their own bowls, and they especially wanted Miss Marvelous.

Round the porch they went, whimpering and

sniffing and poking into corners, hunting a way to get out and go home. They found no way, of course, but they did find the cookie box, empty now and flattened. It still smelled comforting, so they dragged it over to their beds. Then all three curled up on one cushion for company. Each one had a paw or a nose on the bake shop box.

Chapter 4

In the morning, Sally and Jimmie did not wait to dress. They were too anxious to see the dogs. Barefoot and in pajamas, they ran down to the porch. But the dogs still lay snuggled together. They merely rolled mournful eyes at Sally and Jimmie, then looked away.

"Oh! They're even sadder than they were last night," cried Sally.

"I hoped they would have forgotten about being lost. I thought they might be glad to see us this morning and would want to play," said Jimmie.

"Run upstairs and get dressed, children," called Mrs. Henry, coming down to start breakfast. "It's strange we didn't hear from the police officer. We must hurry so we can take the dogs to the police station as soon as possible. Just think how worried their owner must be by this time. How would you feel if you'd lost these three adorable dogs?"

"Maybe they haven't any owner. Then we could keep them, couldn't we?" asked Sally.

"Oh, but they must belong to *some*body," her mother told her.

"Perhaps the owner doesn't want them anymore," said Jimmie.

"I can't imagine anyone not wanting such nice dogs," Mrs. Henry said. "No, children, I think we'll find that someone is very unhappy about their dogs being lost and already is hunting for them. The sooner we get them to the police station the better. Since we're going over to Westville anyway, let's drive to the beach afterwards. And we'll take a picnic lunch. Now then, everybody hurry!"

After that, all was hustle and bustle. Since it was Saturday, Father could go along. There were sandwiches to be made, the lunch basket to be packed, bathing suits and towels had to be gathered and put into the beach bags, and everything had to be loaded into the car.

At last, all was ready. Father and Sally and Jimmie carried the dogs from the house and put them in the big market basket on the floor.

"It's a good place for them to ride," said Sally, climbing into the back seat. "They can be cozy down there all together. I'll pat them every once in a while, too, so they won't feel frightened or lonely."

But the bottom of the basket did not seem cozy to Pumpkin, Ginger, and Spice. They were frightened and lonely. It was not like being in the market basket on the way to the bake shop with Miss Marvelous.

They did not want to be noticed at all now, but today there were no packages for them to hide among. Worst of all, there were no cookies—no warm bake shop smell to make them think they might be going home.

They could not understand what was happening. They wanted Miss Marvelous! It did not help to have Sally pat them and talk to them. They looked as though their little hearts would break.

As the car reached the village, Mrs. Henry said, "I'd like to stop off at the bake shop to get some more of those wonderful ginger cookies for our picnic."

"Good idea," said Mr. Henry. "We'll drop you off there and go on to the police station with the dogs. Then we'll pick you up afterwards."

He brought the car to a stop at the traffic light. Just beyond was the bake shop. It was then that Pumpkin, Ginger, and Spice suddenly sat up, noses in the air, and sniffed very hard.

The light turned green, and Mr. Henry drove across the street and drew up in front of the bake shop.

"Here you are," he said. "Why, look at the dogs! They're all excited! They must have been around here before."

By this time all three dachshunds had their front paws on the edge of the basket. Their eyes were full of eagerness, and their tails began to wave.

Mrs. Henry opened the front door of the car and stepped out. Instantly all three dogs jumped out of the basket and scratched at the back door. They cried and barked to be let out, too.

"See that?" she said. "Something around here certainly must remind them of home."

"Maybe they're just crying because you're leaving them," said Sally, trying hard to pretend that the dogs were beginning to like the Henry family.

"I'm afraid not, dear," said Mother. "They don't really want to stay with us, you know. They want to go wherever it is they belong. But never mind—we promise to see that you get a dog of your own now."

"But I don't want a dog of our own. I want these little brown cookie dogs," said Sally longingly as Mr. Henry drove away.

Mrs. Henry glanced at the bake shop window and stopped, surprised. For there, around the Lazy Susan that Miss Marvelous used to show off special things, was a little dachshund parade—ginger-cookie dachshunds.

"What a strange thing!" thought Mrs. Henry as she went inside. "Just like our overnight visitors. And they seemed to be so fond of ginger cookies, too. I'll get some of those for our picnic. Then perhaps Sally and Jimmie won't feel quite so badly about giving up the real dogs."

Chapter 5

Miss Marvelous came from the warm, sweet-smelling kitchen at one end of the shop to wait on Mrs. Henry. Her eyes were sad, and her voice sounded tired when she asked, "What would you like to have?"

"I'll take some of those adorable cookies in the window," said Mrs. Henry, pointing to the little brown dogs. "I've never seen any like them before."

"I've never made them before," said Miss Marvelous. "You see, I always make cookies to match whatever I'm thinking about—stars and trees at Christmastime, bunnies for Easter, hearts for Saint Valentine's Day, and turkeys for Thanksgiving. In between times, when I have nothing special on my mind, I make just plain round ones. But today I can't seem to think of anything but dachshunds."

"Neither can we!" exclaimed Mrs. Henry. "We've had three of them spending the night with us."

Miss Marvelous looked up quickly. "Three dachshunds spent the night with you? Whose are they?" Her cheeks had turned pink, and her eyes were shining.

"We don't know," said Mrs. Henry. "We found them in the strangest way—in our car! My husband and the children are taking them to . . ."

At that moment the door opened, and in came Mr. Silver and a big, cheerful policeman. Right behind them were Jimmie, Sally, and Mr. Henry with their arms full of wriggling brown dogs.

"Pumpkin! Ginger! Spice!" cried Miss Marvelous.

"Here they are!" Mr. Silver said with a great big smile.

After that, there was great excitement!

There was Miss Marvelous kneeling on the floor, trying to pat all three little brown dogs at once.

There were the dogs, yapping and squealing with joy and climbing all over her to lick her hands and face.

There were the Henrys, all talking at once to tell Miss Marvelous everything that had happened.

There were Mr. Silver and the policeman, standing by and laughing.

Miss Marvelous looked up from patting the dogs.

"When I couldn't find them at home, I thought they had gone to see Mr. Silver. They always have such a good time playing in the woods there. So I went over, and we hunted and called and called and looked all through the woods last night. Then, this morning I phoned the police."

"We never thought of Miss Marvelous' dogs when you called last night," the policeman said to Father. "We somehow thought you'd found the dogs out your way in the country. We don't know all the dogs out there so well."

"I guess I didn't make it clear that my wife and children had been here in Westville and found them in the back of the car when they got back home," said Father. "We're renting a house in Easttown for the summer. We come here to the market and go to the beach."

"We tried to reach you on the telephone just after Miss Marvelous reported her three were lost," answered the policemen, "but you were already on your way here, I suppose."

In a few moments, Mr. Silver said, "I must hurry to tell Polly and Jack the dogs are found. They've been hunting as hard as the rest of us. This is something to celebrate with another ice cream party, all right!"

He patted Pumpkin, Ginger, and Spice before he left.

As soon as things quieted down a little, Mrs. Henry said, "It was because of the ginger cookies we bought here yesterday that they jumped into our car. They smelled the Marvelous Bake Shop smell—and we never guessed!"

"Of course," said Miss Marvelous. "That must have been it."

"They're such nice dogs. We wish they were ours," said Jimmie.

"Oh yes," said Sally, patting them as they huddled happily close to Miss Marvelous' feet. "But they don't seem to like us very much."

"That's just because they were homesick," Miss Marvelous told her. "You children must come visit them at my house. Then you'll see—they'll make friends right away and want to play with you."

"Oh, can we?" cried Jimmie.

"We'd love that," said Sally. "We haven't any dog at home, you know."

Mr. Henry spoke up, "No, we haven't, but we want one, and we're going to see about getting one now."

"Oh!" said Miss Marvelous. "Ohhhh!" And suddenly she sounded mysterious. "So you want a dog, do you? And I suppose you wish it could be a dog like these."

Sally and Jimmie nodded.

"Well now, if you don't mind waiting a little while, you can have one of Spice's puppies."

"Really? Truly?" shouted Sally and Jimmie at once.

"Yes, as soon as they're born, I'll let you choose the one you like the best. Then, when it's old enough to leave its mother, you can take it home to keep for your very own. It will be a thank-you puppy—a present for taking such good care of my dogs."

"Oh!" said Sally breathlessly. "How wonderful!"

"Miss Marvelous is marvelous!" shouted Jimmie.

Suddenly everybody laughed and laughed and laughed.

Miss Marvelous wiped her eyes with her handkerchief.

"Here's a little present in the meantime," she said. She gave Sally and Jimmie and all of the grownups three dachshund cookies each. "You all helped bring the dogs back to me!"

Everybody thanked Miss Marvelous.

And Sally said, "Next time we're in Westville, we'll come see Pumpkin, Ginger, and Spice." She turned at the door to stroke each one for the last time.

"And soon we'll have Syrup!" said Jimmie, whirling around on his heel.

For a moment everyone looked puzzled.

"Syrup?" asked Sally. "Oh, I know. You mean our own dog—the thank-you puppy! That's a sweet name!"

"Sweet as syrup," said the policeman as he followed the Henry family out of the bake shop, each carrying dachshund cookies.

"Sweet as Pumpkin, Ginger, and Spice!" called Miss Marvelous after them.

As the Henrys got into their car, they all looked back at her smiling in the doorway. At her feet, the three little brown dogs waved their tails to say goodbye.

THE END